Annabelle's Secrets

I remember it well, the farmhouse. She didn't want to go. Her parents didn't understand, they never did. It was the secrets. She never told them, she never wanted to. But I knew. Annabelle had a gift, it was a gift she didn't want. The kind that kept you up at night sending cold shivers down your spine. The kind that made your hair stand. Always making you look over your shoulder. You know that feeling you have when you are alone. It's deep down in your gut. It's them, they have always been there. You can't see them but Annabelle can. It's scary at times, the scream's I mean. It's sudden, at night. This time was different. My mom just died and she was here for the funeral. It was summer, she always stayed for the summer, she was my cousin. We had never moved and my dad had always had this farm. A house and a barn and an old tire that swung from the tree. She stood by the swing watching as my dad talked to the priest. I knew they were talking about her, they always did. It was as if they had a fear that something was going to happen, something bad. I didn't want to think about it, I never did. Annabelle was fifteen the same age as me. I watched as she stared, looking as if she was in a daze. Appearing almost lifeless and pale. I walked slowly toward her, I knew this had to be hard for her, it was hard for me. I called out her name quietly as I stood behind her. Waiting to hear a response. There was nothing, not one sound. She just stood there staring. I could hear her breathing. The hair on my arms started to stand. I hated when she was like this. I called her name again this time a little louder, with more urgency in my voice. She slowly turned and stared at me. Her eyes glazed over. "They're here!" she said quietly.

I looked over at my dad, I was sure she was talking about the priest. Annabelle hated when he was around. He was always asking her questions about the things she was saying. I couldn't blame her though, I hated for people to ask me things too. But this was different, these questions were not the same. I turned back but Annabelle had already walked to the porch. Her room was upstairs, right down the hall from mine. I didn't want to go in, I just wanted to be alone for a while. I wanted everyone to just leave. I knew that wasn't going to happen so I turned toward the swing. It was swaying back and forth as if someone had just swung in it. I looked back at the house Annabelle was staring out of the upstairs window, then she was gone. I felt uneasy again, as if I was being watched. I'm sure you've had the same feeling, as if he's right behind you breathing on your neck, you can feel him but you can't see him. He's there though you can feel it. He's watching you, touching you. I had chores that needed to be done. Around the farm there were always things that had to be done. I just wanted to keep busy, keep my mind off the things that were really going on. Keep my mind off of Annabelle most of all. The funeral would be over soon but I knew Annabelle would still be here. She had to stay in the summer with us. Her parents were always really busy with work during the summer. I never understood why they had to leave so much and why Annabelle always had to stay with us, I didn't like it.

It's like having that annoying little cousin around that you don't want following you no more. Except she wasn't following me, she was scaring me. It Makes me feel uneasy every time I see her. When she was around I didn't even want to go inside, I didn't want to go to sleep. You will see. You will start to feel uneasy, just like I did. I remember my dad calling for me. When I went to see what he wanted I noticed that everyone was leaving, I was glad. It was going to be a long night and I just wanted to be left alone. I remember my dad putting his arm around me as we went into the house. Telling me that I needed to eat and that Annabelle needed to come down stairs. Telling me that we all needed to be a family right now and that we would get through it together, but that's not what I wanted. I didn't want to be a family right now. I just wanted to be left alone with my dad. Why couldn't it just be the two of us, why couldn't Annabelle stay with her parents right now. There were a lot of things that I didn't understand and Annabelle was one of them. Maybe I would never understand her. This was one summer that I would never forget. It all started right after my mom died. Why did it have to start then? Why did it have to happen? There were so many questions, I still have them. I still wonder what it would have been like if she would not have been there. Would things have turned out differently. I'll never know and neither will you. What I did know is that Annabelle was still here and I had to go upstairs soon. I had to go to sleep and this time my mom would not be here. Have you ever felt alone, afraid of the dark? Have you ever been woken up, feeling like you're being watched. I did all the time. I was starting to feel cold. Was I getting sick? I remember quickly eating then I started upstairs, I was tired. I didn't see Annabelle anywhere, I was glad. I fell asleep fast, then I heard it. I was woken by it. I didn't want to move or make a sound. I just wanted it to go away. I could feel the hair on my neck started to stand. I was still cold, I could see my breath. My room was dark. Just a small light from the hall could be seen from underneath my bedroom door. It was the same sound I heard every night. I didn't know who it was or what it was. I was always afraid to go look but tonight was different. Tonight Annabelle was here. I had that feeling again, the one deep down in the gut of my stomach. I walked slowly towards my room door reaching out for the door knob slowly pulling it open. I looked towards the stairs then back down the hall. The only thing I could see was the breath in front of me. The house was silent and dark. I turned towards my room again and that's when I saw her, standing, staring down the hall. She was wearing her white nightgown, her hair dark and small strands covering her eyes. "She's here!" Annabelle said slowly in a low voice. I didn't want to hear it. I went back into my room and closed the door. I remember waking up the next morning. The sun was shining through the window in my room. I couldn't hear anything but the birds outside. I got up and looked out the window. It was the priest again. He was talking to Annabelle outside. He always came by and talked to her, I wasn't sure why. It happened every summer and it was always about the same time in the morning. I stepped out on the porch so I could hear them. Father Stevens was his name. He was about middle aged and had known our family for a long time. I loved going to church, I hadn't been in a long time. I'm not sure why we quit going.

"I always come to see them," Annabelle said. "Who, who do you come to see?" Father Stevens asked. "I come every year, I don't want to," Annabelle said. "But they need me to," she replied. "Who needs you to?"

Father Stevens asked. Annabelle looked at me. "I got to go!" she screamed out. Father Stevens watched as she ran in the house. He stood staring at me, I quickly went back in. Annabelle was standing in the living room. "What did he want?" I asked. She didn't say anything. Just quickly went back upstairs. I was confused, I looked back out the window. Father Stevens was still standing staring at the house. I felt a hand touch my shoulder. It startled me for a minute, it was my dad. He didn't say anything just stood there staring out the window. We watched as Father Stevens walked down the road until he was out of sight. There were still two more days until the funeral. I just wanted it to be over. I wanted Annabelle to go back home. I walked back up the stairs, Annabelle was in her room. I stood at her door and watched her for a minute. She was sitting on her bed facing the mirror. "I saw her again last night," she said. I didn't say anything. I didn't want to talk to her about it. I just turned and went back to my room. Why did she have to be here? Things were hard enough without her being here. I saw a shadow pass my room. You know the ones you see out of the corner of your eye. The ones that come and go as fast as you see them. I'm sure you see them, we all do. Most of us just shrug them off. As if to say it's our imagination, well it's not. Just wait and you will see it too. You will see what I'm talking about. It's them they have always been there, I didn't know it but now I do. I can't see them, but I know they are there. I didn't want to hear about it. I didn't want to be told. All I wanted was to be left alone, by myself. I thought about staying in my room all day but I didn't want that either. I didn't want to be reminded of the things that had happened. I decided that I would go out and swing, enjoy the morning air.

It's something that me and my mother always did. We always went and swung in the morning right before we would start our chores. There was lots to be done on the farm. There were still lots that I needed to do. I walked out by the old tree. When I got there the swing was swaying back and forth again. I just stood there staring at it. Annabelle walked up beside me. She didn't say anything. She just stood there staring like me. "I miss her," I replied. Annabelle didn't say anything back. She didn't have to. I knew that she heard me and that's all that mattered. I watched as the swing swayed. Caught in my memories I didn't even notice that Annabelle had left, as if she was never there. Have you ever lost anyone? It's as if everything you do you always see them. Like a record playing over and over but you never seem to get to the end. As if the last song is never played. I can still see her, I know she's with me. I heard Annabelle talking again, it was the priest who came back. I didn't know why he hung around so much, he always wanted to talk to Annabelle.

 "I came by to invite you Sunday," Father Stevens said. "It would be good to get away for awhile," he replied. "They need me here, I can't leave yet," Annabelle replied. "I need to help my cousin, there's still a lot to be done, I don't think you would understand" she explained. "I don't see anyone, where's your cousin?" Father Stevens asked. "Sometimes people need your help, they don't know they need help but they do," Annabelle explained. "I don't want to be here but I have to be," she replied. "Why do you have to be here?" Father Stevens asked. "To help them, I see them all the time, everywhere. I'm the only one that can help them" Annabelle explained. "I have to go now, you can come back later" Annabelle replied.

She always kept busy around the farm when she was here. I didn't need her help and I didn't want it. My mom always said the more help the better but I just didn't want Annabelle here. It was the things she said and did that scared me. You will see, I did. It all started when she was younger, she didn't come to our house back then. She didn't start coming to our house until a couple of years ago when her mom and dad got their new job. My mom said it was going to be a temporary thing but she started coming and hasn't stopped since. Sometimes I wish I could just tell her to leave. I wish things could go back to the way they were. Have you ever wanted to change things? I do all the time. I would change everything. Maybe I could just talk to Annabelle, maybe I could get her to understand how I felt. I don't know if that would change anything but I wanted to try. Maybe if I talked to her maybe she would just leave. "Annabelle, I know why you are here. I know why you came, I miss her to" I replied. Annabelle was sitting in the flower bed, her hand running over each flower as if she was in a daze. I wondered what thoughts were running through her mind. Was it the same as mine? Did she miss her as much as I did? I watched as Annabelle got up and went inside, she still didn't respond.

"Hello, I know you are here" Annabelle said as she slowly walked through the living room. "I'm not afraid, let me help you," Annabelle replied. It was the same feeling that you have when you are alone. You know that you're being watched, you know that he's there. You can't see him but Annabelle can. Annabelle went back upstairs to her room, she sat on the bed again facing the mirror. "It wasn't your fault," she replied. "You don't have to be afraid," Annabelle said. The room was growing colder and Annabelle sat watching her breath rise in front of her. "I know what you need," she replied. Her room door slammed shut behind her and Annabelle squeezed her eyes shut tight. "It wasn't your fault, it wasn't your fault, it wasn't your fault" she kept saying over and over. You know that feeling you get when someone reaches out from behind you and grabs you. That feeling that just takes over you from nowhere. Annabelle was expecting it but it never happened, she just sat there repeating herself expecting something, anything to happen. But nothing ever did. Annabelle opened her eyes and that's when she saw him, she let out a horrible scream, it frightened her. He was beside her bed bent over looking down at her with a huge smile. "Annabelle!" he said in a slow voice. Frightened, she scooted backwards falling off the bed and landing on the floor. All she could do was stare at him. And he looked at her with the awfulest grin. "Annabelle!" he said again in a slow voice. Annabelle quickly got up and swung her room door open running down the stairs and out to the porch. "Annabelle" a voice said as a hand reached out and grabbed her shoulder. She screamed again, still frightened from before. "Father Stevens" Annabelle replied. "What are you doing here?" Annabelle asked. "I was just passing when I heard you screaming" Father Stevens replied. "Is everything alright?" he asked. Annabelle didn't say a word. She just stood there staring at the priest. "Let's go take a walk," Father Stevens said. Staring into the house he had an uneasy feeling about what may be inside. "I used to walk this dirt road all the time," Annabelle said. "I used to come out here when I felt alone, scared, or just had nothing better to do," she replied. "Have you ever been scared?" she asked Father Stevens. There are times when I get scared, yes" he explained. "I get scared sometimes but I know they need my help" Annabelle explained. "Who needs your help Annabelle?" Father Stevens asked. "Annabelle you're starting to scare me," Father Stevens said. "I talk to them all the time, sometimes I do get scared," she replied. "It's the house isn't it" Father Stevens asked. Annabelle didn't say anything. "Annabelle, I need to tell you something," Father Stevens replied. "I don't want to scare you but I think that you should know," he replied. "Ten years ago I performed an exorcism in that house for your family. It was on a five year old girl, after the exorcism she was never seen again" Father Stevens explained. "There's more things that happened as well," Father Stevens said. "I think I know what you mean," Annabelle replied. "I may have been young but I have heard some stories. I have also seen some things, some things that you might not understand" Annabelle replied. "Annabelle you have to promise me that you will not say anything" Father Stevens said. "You come around here a lot," Annabelle replied. "You don't have to, they don't want you to," Annabelle said. "Who doesn't want me to Annabelle?" Father Stevens asked. "You know that feeling you get when you're alone, I get it all the time" Annabelle said. "I have to go now, you need to go now!" Annabelle said. "They don't want you around here" she screamed as she ran through the yard. I didn't understand why Annabelle got so upset all the time. She never got upset around my mom. She had a way with people, with words. I was never really good with words. In fact, I had a hard time expressing myself. I prefered to just be left alone. Maybe that's why I had a hard time around Annabelle. My mom always told me that the words would come to just be patient and wait. Patience is something I didn't have. Not even when I was younger. And I certainly didn't have the patience to wait until summer was over. Every year it was the same thing over and over. Annabelle would come and stay and my mom would say how happy she was to see her and they would spend all this time together. But still it always seemed as if something was missing. I'm sure you have had that feeling. There were times when it was just my mom.I enjoyed those times. I wish there could have been more of them. There was more than just this farm. We took walks and went to church and there were blackberries on the hill we picked all the time. All the memories I had just kept playing over and over in my head. I tried to stay busy but it didn't help. I tried to stay away from Annabelle but that wasn't helping either. There was still something missing, something out of place. I decided I would try to talk to Annabelle again. Maybe the things my mom told me were right after all, maybe I just needed to have patience. Annabelle was swinging on the old tire swing. She always seemed to be in such a daze. I just stood watching her, I didn't say anything.

 "It's happening again," Annabelle said quietly. She quit moving the swing and just stared at me. It was starting to scare me. She just kept staring as if someone was standing behind me or maybe I was the problem. I wanted to tell Annabelle how I felt, she needed to know but I couldn't say anything I just stood there. I remember closing my eyes tight. Thinking that this was all a nightmare, a nightmare that I was living. Hoping that when I opened my eyes back up that this would all be over, that everything would be different. "It wasn't your fault," Annabelle said quietly. I opened my eyes back up and Annabelle was standing next to the swing. "It wasn't your fault" she said again. I watched as Annabelle went back into the house. I didn't say anything. I didn't know what to say. I had never heard Annabelle say that before. So many things had happened. I was afraid and confused. Maybe this all will be over soon. I know that nothing will be the same, things will never go back to the way they were. So many things were lost. I remember standing there and thinking. All this time Annabelle had been coming around. For years she had been at this farm, every summer. Saying things and doing things that scared me all the time. Sometimes I think that she did it on purpose. She knew I didn't like her being here. She knew I didn't like her saying the things that she said but she did them anyway. I didn't want to think about it any more. I didn't want to think about what had happened. Why did Annabelle have to be here? I went back into the house. I needed to just go lay down in my room, forget about everything. But that's not what happened. I remember going upstairs and that's when I saw her, Annabelle I mean. She was in my parents room, she was holding a small bracelet in her hands. "What are you doing?" I yelled at her. "Where did you get that?" I asked. Annabelle just stood there staring at the bracelet, holding it in her hands, rubbing its smooth sides. "It was hers," she replied. "It's been here the whole time," she said. "It's all happening again," Annabelle said. "Put it back," I said staring at Annabelle. I wasn't sure what she was going to do. "It wasn't your fault" Annabelle said again. "You were young, just a kid," she replied. "You weren't supposed to be there," she said quietly. "It wasn't supposed to happen," she said quietly again. "You have to promise me not to tell," Annabelle said. Have you ever had someone ask you to keep a secret, something important. That's what

Annabelle just did. I didn't know what to do. I was scared. "Conner you have to promise me" Annabelle said. "Alright" I said as Annabelle walked past me down the hall to her room. She still had the bracelet, what was I going to say. Something didn't feel right but it never did with Annabelle around. I remember thinking what if she got caught.

She wasn't supposed to be in my parents room but it didn't matter now. It had been a very long time since I saw that bracelet and I didn't like the fact that Annabelle now had it. So many memories were being brought back up. Things that I tried to forget, things that I didn't want to remember but I didn't have a choice now. I didn't know how to stop it. Annabelle was the reason for all this. So many things I tried to hide inside. I heard the door downstairs shut. I didn't want to be caught in my parents room so I decided to go to mine. Annabelle's room was at the top of the stairs then it was mine and my parents. We had a small bathroom at the corner we all had to share. That was always fun in the mornings. I remember laying down on my bed. Thinking about what Annabelle had said. I knew I couldn't control things that happen but still I couldn't help but wonder if things would have been different if she had never been here. I kept thinking about what Annabelle said, It's happening again. How would she know anyway? It's in the past and it didn't matter anymore. You can't fix things in the past. This was Annabelle trying to scare me again. Saying things that she knew would bother me. Trying to get her way. Well it wasn't going to work this time. I wasn't going to listen. I started to close my eyes when I saw it again, the shadow I mean. You only see them out of the corner of your eye. The ones that you see, I know you do. It went right past my room, towards

Annabelle's room. Only this time it wasn't at night. I slowly got up from my bed. The house was quiet. I walked slowly towards my room door peering out into the hall. I didn't see anything. I remember taking a deep breath and slowly walking towards Annabelle's room. I stopped just outside her door. Annabelle was sitting on her bed with her back facing the door. I could see her holding out the bracelet in her hand. Why was she still looking at it? I remember thinking to myself. I couldn't see anything else. I went back to my room and laid down and closed my eyes. I just wanted this day to be over with. I wanted to hurry up and get the funeral over, Have you ever wanted something to just hurry up. Have you ever just wanted time to pass but the more you think about it the more it just stands still. I didn't want to go to sleep. I didn't even remember going to sleep. But I did and it happened again. I was woken by it again. This time it was more clear. It was louder and sounded like it was closer. I looked around my room and it was dark. How long was I asleep for I remember thinking. I was cold again. I had to be getting sick. My room door was shut, I didn't remember shutting it. I looked over at my clock, it was three in the morning. Did I really sleep that long I thought to myself. The small light was coming from under my door again. I wanted to get up and go check on Annabelle. I slowly opened my door and looked down the hall. I didn't see anything. I slowly stepped out of my room and looked over the banister. That's when I saw her, Annabelle I mean. She was slowly coming up the stairs. Wearing her white nightgown again. Small strands of hair covering her face again. I couldn't see her eyes. I quickly moved back into my room again and closed the door. I could hear Annabelle. "It wasn't your fault," she said slowly. Was she talking to me? I remember standing with my back to the door listening. The sounds I heard were more clearer tonight but I still could not make out what it was. I could see my breath in front of me, my heart pounding. Something didn't seem right. Annabelle didn't seem right. I kept listening but I couldn't hear anything. I was afraid to open the door and look. I knelt down in front of the door and that's when I saw it. The bracelet was sitting on my nightstand beside my bed. Was Annabelle in my room. Had she came here when I was sleeping. I slowly got up and walked to my night stand. There it was right in front of me. I reached down to pick it up. There was something written on the inside. I couldn't make it out. I didn't want to turn the light on so I walked over to the window. I could just make it out from the light of the moon, Claireabelle. I dropped the bracelet on the floor and took a couple steps back. I could feel someone behind me, touching me. I could feel them breathing on my neck. I felt something on my right shoulder. I slowly turned to look, it was someone's hand sliding across my shoulder, touching my neck. I don't remember anything after that. I woke up the next morning in my bed. The bracelet was gone. What had happened, who was in my room? Where did the bracelet go? Annabelle I remember thinking. Where was Annabelle? She wasn't in her room. Something wasn't right. I remember asking my dad where Annabelle was. He said she was alright and that she would be back. I remember him telling me that I didn't look alright. Asking me how I felt. He said he needed to call Dr. Richards to come and check on me. I didn't want that. I didn't want to go through any of that anymore. I asked him about the bracelet, about Claireabelle. He just stared at me, told me that there was nothing here that belonged to

Claireablle and that he was calling Dr. Richards immediately. I had been through all this before. I had put everything behind me. It was Annabelle's fault all of this. It wouldn't be happening if she was not here. I didn't want to talk to Dr. Richards again. I wasn't going crazy. I know what I saw, what I heard. My parents called Dr. Richards when I was little. They said I needed help coping with everything. He always came once a week and we would talk for an hour then he would talk with my parents. He told them I struggled with depression and I would have a hard time coping with traumatic events in my life. I knew what he was thinking. Just because my mom died didn't mean I was having a hard time coping. He wasn't listening to me. He didn't believe what I was telling him. Dr. Richards talked to me about everything that had happened. As I got older he told my parents that he didn't think it was necessary to come around anymore. And if I had a relapse then they could call him and he would come back out. But I wasn't having a relapse. I needed to talk to Annabelle. Where was she? Dr. Richards would ask me how I was doing and how I was feeling. I would have to go through all the emotions with him. Usually I was feeling afraid. I was young then. I told him what I heard and what I saw. The truth is that I still hear it at night. It still frightens me. I don't know what it is and I'm afraid to go look. But that is all changing now. Annabelle is here now. Dr. Richards tried to make me forget about everything. Told me that everything was going to be all right from now on and that I didn't have anything else that I needed to worry about. He would usually record our sessions and take notes. He was always very precise about what he asked. I didn't want to tell him everything. I was always afraid of what might happen if I did.

There were so many things that had happened. I went back to my room, I wanted to look for the bracelet. I searched everywhere. Then I went to Annabelle's room. I couldn't find the bracelet anywhere. I heard someone coming down the hall, it was Annabelle. "What are you doing here?" she asked. "Why are you in my room?" Annabelle demanded to know. "It's all your fault, everything!" I screamed out. "Nothing would happen if you were not here" I screamed. "Give me that bracelet!" I demanded. "Give it to me now!" I screamed. Annabelle just stood staring at me. She didn't say anything but she needed to know how I felt. I remember my dad pulling me away from Annabelle and telling me that Dr. Richards was there and that I needed to go talk to him Immediately. He pulled me downstairs and into the living room and told me to sit on the couch. I needed to find that bracelet. Annabelle was hiding something, I knew she was. Dr. Richards was much older now. He looked nothing like I had remembered. He dressed very professionally. He was in his sixties now, had grey hair around the sides of his head but the top was going bald. He had a very well trimmed beard and wore a watch on his right hand that he always kept the time with. "Hello Conner, it's been awhile" Dr. Richards said. I didn't say anything. "I'm sorry about your mother Conner, would you like to talk about it." he asked. "This is not about my mother," I replied. "What do you remember about her?" he asked,over looking at what I had said. "My mother was nice, she wouldn't be letting any of this happen" I replied. Dr. Richards just sat watching me, holding the pen and notepad. "My mother tried to stop it all. She didn't want any of this to happen. She was kind. I wasn't supposed to be there. I wasn't supposed to see anything. I couldn't help it. I remember my mom wearing her pink and white dress. She had on her gold necklace. She told me everything would be alright. Well everything is not alright!" I explained to Dr. Richards. He didn't say anything. Just kept writing in his notepad. "Annabelle has Claireabelle's bracelet" I slowly replied. Dr. Richards looked up from his notepad. "Conner we have been over this" Dr. Richards said. "I think we should start meeting again, on a regular basis," Dr. Richards replied. He went back to writing in his notepad. "I saw it, I'm not going crazy," I replied. "Annabelle has it, I know she does!" I yelled out. "I'm going to write out a prescription for you to take, to help you calm down" Dr. Richards said. "You can take it before you go to sleep, it will help you sleep," he explained. "Can you tell me what your mother was like Conner " Dr. Richards asked. "We always went on walks and swung in the mornings. She would always read to us at night and we would go to church on sundays. After church we would go and pick berries. My mother was nice and I don't want to talk about it anymore!" I replied. Dr. Richards looked up from the notepad and stared at me for a moment. "That will be all for now Conner" he replied. I watched as he went and talked with my dad. After he left I went back upstairs. Annabelle was sitting in her room. "Where is the bracelet?" I asked. Annabelle turned and looked at me. "You promised me," she replied. "She was here," she said. "In your room, she was watching you," Annabelle said quietly. "She still has the scars across her face, she was behind you, touching you, she's drawn to you" Annabelle said. "You're lying!" I said as I walked to my room. I didn't want to hear anymore. This was Annabelle trying to say things to scare me again. Still I couldn't help but wonder who was in my room last night and where the bracelet went. My father was always quick to call Dr. Richards. My mom didn't like it. He always said I had problems that needed to be dealt with. We were never close. He always seemed distant, like he was trying to hide things. He even acted strange at times. My mom always told me not to worry about it. Said I was too young to be worrying about things. Things were different now. Now I had to get used to my mom not being here. I had to get used to my dad and what was even worse than that is that I had to get used to Annabelle. Something was going on. I didn't know what it was but it scared me a little. I needed to find that bracelet. I was sure if I found it a lot would be explained. I didn't believe what Annabelle was saying and I decided I wasn't taking any medication. I needed to be awake, alert to what was really happening. I needed to know what was going on, who was in my room and why Annabelle was acting so strange. I was sure something wasn't right. Still everything seemed so familiar, like I had seen it all before. I lay there in my bed trying to put it all together, the sounds that I heard at night, the events that took place. Still I could not figure it out. All I could think about was the bracelet, it had to have something to do with all this. It was being hidden and kept from me. Why was Annabelle telling me these things? What did she know? I decided that I was going to write down the events that had happened. Try to figure all this out. I pulled out my journal from the desk in my room and started writing. I was careful to write each date and time that the events were taking place. The screams I heard at night, seeing Annabelle in the hall, someone being in my room, the priest arriving everyday. I was careful not to miss anything that I saw or heard. I just kept writing and writing. When I was done I started from the beginning reading everything that I had written. Every word, every time, every sentence and that's when I noticed it. It was like deja vu. Like a record playing over and over again. The events were happening at the same time every night. The screams, Annabelle in the hall, what did it all mean. I could start to feel my breath shorten. I was feeling scared. What was going on and what did it have to do with me? I quickly put the journal down and pushed myself away from the desk. I had to talk to the priest. Annabelle talked to him everyday. He had to know something that was going on. I didn't like this feeling, not knowing what was happening and what was going on. It was as if everyone was hiding something from me, something from the past. I was having that feeling again as if I was alone. Deceived from my own past. But how, something was missing. Something very important. I went outside and sat on the swing. It was almost time for the priest to come by. I waited patiently, watching to see if I was correct. Letting the events play over and over in my mind and that's when I noticed him. Father Stevens was walking down the road. I quickly got up and ran towards him. "Father Stevens" I said as I ran up to him. "We have to talk, can we take a walk?" I asked quickly. "Conner" he replied in amazement. "It's been a long time," he said. "Father I have to ask you some things and I need you to tell me the truth" I replied. "Conner, I am a priest," Father Stevens said. "Something is happening again and I think that Annabelle has something to do with it," I explained. "It's strange and hard to explain but there are screams at night and Annabelle is acting weird and she had Claireabelles bracelet," I said. Father Stevens stopped walking and stared at me for a moment. "Claireabelle, are you sure?" he asked. "I saw it," I replied. "Everyone keeps telling me that I'm going crazy, I'm not crazy, I know what I saw" I replied. "My mom's funeral is just a day away and now all this is happening, something is not right" I replied. Father Stevens just stood there staring at me with a blank look on his face. "Father what's wrong?" I asked. He stood there staring at me for a minute "Conner your mom has been dead for several years now!" he replied. I felt my heart stop, I couldn't breath. I just stared at him for a moment. "NO! NO! That's not true!" I screamed. "Conner it's the house, it's all happening again. I was afraid of this, you're not safe there Conner! She didn't tell you?" the priest asked. "Conner! Conner! Look at me!" the priest yelled. "Who didn't tell me?" I asked. I could feel my chest start to tighten. It was getting harder to breath. "I was afraid of this," the priest replied. "I have to get you somewhere safe, it's all happening again" the priest explained. "NO! NO!" I screamed out. "I can't leave, I have to know what is going on" I screamed out as I ran back towards the house. The priest just stood watching, staring back towards the house. What was happening to me? Why could I not remember what happened? This is not the way I remember any of this. Something was missing, missing from my memory. Everything was happening so fast. I tried to think, I had to remember. I ran straight upstairs to my parents room, my dad had left, this was my chance to look around. Everything looked the same, my mom's clothes were still hanging in the closet and her pictures were everywhere. Nothing made sense to me. Annabelle was still in her room with the door shut. I tried to think, what was I missing? I slowly went down the stairs into the kitchen. I looked around at everything. Then I remembered one of the sessions I had with Dr Richards when I was younger. I turned around slowly and there it was. I had forgotten about it. It was the door to the basement. I never went down there anymore, I never thought about it. I felt uneasy again, like I was being watched. I stared at the door for a moment. Did I really want to go back down there I remember thinking. So many memories I had forgotten. I took a deep breath and started walking towards the door slowly. "Conner!" a voice shouted from behind me. It startled me and I jumped a little. It was my dad. "I didn't hear you come in," I replied. I watched as he put his satchel down on the counter. The basement was going to have to wait for now. "Don't you have chores that need to be done?" he said staring at me. "Yes sir" I replied. He watched as I slowly went past him, I looked back before I went out and Annabelle was standing at the balcony, watching everything that was happening. I knew Annabelle was hiding something and after talking to the priest I knew she was hiding a lot. I had to find out what secrets she had. Maybe I needed to listen to what she was telling me. Annabelle had said it was all happening again and so did the priest. What did they know that I did not? I remember finishing up my chores, it was getting late. When I went inside I quickly ate dinner and my dad handed me a glass of water and a pill. I put it in my mouth and quickly drank the water and hurried upstairs to my room closing the door behind me. I opened the window to my room and spit the pill out. I remember thinking that I needed to be alert tonight. I needed to know what was going on. I quickly got in bed and layed there thinking. It was dark and quiet and it seemed like forever before I heard my dad coming up the stairs. I could hear the footsteps in the hall and they stopped just outside my door. I quickly closed my eyes as I heard the door to my room slowly open and a few seconds later shut again. I was sure he was checking to see if the medicine had put me to sleep. It was only eight o'clock. After that night Dr. Richards came to the house every week. "Conner It's good to see you again" Dr. Richards said. "I thought we would do things a little different today," he explained. "Conner I would like to talk about your childhood. Things that you did when you were younger. Can we talk about that?" Dr. Richards asked. I remember thinking that I didn't want to talk about anything but that was going to be the only way to get him to quit coming around. "Sure" I replied. "Let's talk about my childhood." Dr. Richards stared at me for a second. "Conner what do you remember about your childhood, growing up in this house" he asked. "I remember Annabelle didn't come around as often, it was better like that" I said. "You don't like Annabelle much do you Conner?" Dr. Richards asked. "I don't like the way she stares at me, I don't like the way she talks to me and I don't like the lies!" I said. "We will get back to that, I want to focus on when you were younger. What do you remember?" Dr. Richards asked. "It was just me and my parents. We always went to church on sundays. Mom would always chase me through the house playing and Dad was always working. Things were different then. I could always talk to my mom, you were never around" I replied. "My mom was not the only one that would play. There were times that Annabelle did come around, we would play hide and go seek. Do you remember playing hide and go seek when you were little? I can still remember searching for her, calling for her. Annabelle! I would say, slowly, quietly, as I slowly searched. Annabelle! I would say. Do you really want to know about my childhood Dr. Richards?" I asked. "Stop writing and answer me!" I said. I remember Dr. Richards slowly looked up at me then he continued to write. "There was someone else. We were not alone, we were never alone. Annabelle always hid her and would never tell me where. She had the best hiding spot. I could have looked for hours and I would have never found her. Were you ever good at playing hide and go seek? I was never good at hiding and was always the one searching. Sometimes I feel like I'm still searching. Have you ever felt like you were searching for something and could never find it?" I asked. "That was not the first time we played hide and go seek, there were many other times to. I didn't understand what was going on then. Claireabelle would mumble things to herself and when I asked her what was wrong she would scream and cover her eyes. It was frightening, she scared us. She kept screaming leave me alone, leave me alone. I didn't know what to do, what was I supposed to do?" I replied. I remember breathing faster and faster my heart was pounding. "Conner! Conner!" Dr. Richards screamed. He had a hold of my shoulders and was shaking me. "Conner! It's all right!" he replied. I remember just sitting there staring at him. All the emotions were running through my head. All the memories I had tried to forget were racing through my mind all at once. "Conner what happened to your sister was not your fault!" Dr. Richards said. "My sister!" I replied. "I think that will be enough for now," Dr. Richards said as he went to talk with my dad. There were many more sessions after that. Talking with Dr. Richards had become a regular routine again. Except I wasn't taking my medication any more. "Conner, I have asked Steven your father to sit in on our discussion today, is that alright?" Dr. Richards asked. "Alright" I replied. I remembered this particular conversation better than the rest. "Conner, I would like to talk about Claireabelle," Dr. Richards said. I was starting to feel it again deep down in my gut but I wasn't alone. I was feeling cold, like I was getting sick. "Conner," Dr. Richards said again. I just sat there for a min, in a daze, I didn't know what to say. "Conner, can you tell me what happened to your sister?" Dr. Richards asked. "My sister?" I said quietly. Dr. Richards looked over at my father for a moment then back at me. "Conner, are you feeling alright?" Dr. Richards asked. He just sat there and stared at me for a minute. "Conner what happened to Claireabelle?" he asked. "She was screaming, screaming, all I could hear were her screams!" I said. I could feel my heart beating. "Conner what was she screaming for?" Dr. Richards asked. Have you ever felt like something was wrong with you but you didn't know what it was? As if you were being pulled into every direction at once. My mind was racing, all the thoughts were running through at one time. "It wasn't your fault!" I heard a voice say. I turned quickly to look, it was Annabelle. "What happened wasn't your fault Conner! You were young and scared and so was I" she replied. "We should have never been down there. Conner you went back didn't you! You were trying to search for her!" Annabelle shouted. "Annabelle, that's enough," Dr. Richards said. "You will never find her" Annabelle shouted. I watched as my dad got up and pulled Annabelle out of the room. She was hiding things from me. I knew it, all this time there were secrets being kept from me. Why could I not remember what was happening. It had to be because of Dr. Richards and maybe my dad was involved as well. All I could think was if my mom was here things would be different. "Conner," Dr. Richards said again. "It is important that you can tell me what happened that night," he explained. "What happened to Claireablle?" he asked. "I don't know" I blurted out. "She just kept screaming and covering her eyes as if something or someone was messing with her, she kept screaming leave me alone but no one was messing with her, no one was touching her. It's in this house isn't it Dr. Richards! You feel it, don't you!" I screamed out. I don't know what took over me, I was feeling upset, I remember it well. I was scared and angry and confused."That's all for today Conner" he said as he watched me quickly leave the room. "It's happening again" Annabelle said as she came back in staring at Dr. Richards. "I've seen this before, with Claireabelle," Annabelle said. "I watched it and I couldn't do anything to help her, well not this time!" Annabelle replied. "I can see them, there everywhere! I'm the only one that can help them!" Annabelle replied. "Who do you see Annabelle?" Dr. Richards asked as he motioned for Annabelle to sit down. "I can see Aunt Sarah, She's beautiful," Annnabelle replied. "Sarah has been dead for several years Annabelle" Dr. Richards said. "I don't have the bracelet, I gave it back" Annabelle replied. "Conner has to know the truth, he has to know what is going on," Annabelle replied. "You can't keep him like this forever, he has to know," Annabelle explained. "I've been talking to Father stevens." Dr. Richards stood up. "You've been what?" Dr. Richards asked. "Annabelle this was to have never been brought back up! What have you done? What have you said?" Dr. Richards asked. "Father Stevens already knows, he was there!" Annabelle replied. "It doesn't matter!" Dr. Richards yelled. "I will take care of this! You are to say nothing more!" he instructed as he walked out of the room. It wasn't fair. Conner has to know the truth.

"Annabelle... Annabelle!" the voice said from behind her. She didn't turn to look. Just sat there breathing slowly. She could feel him behind her, she could see him looking at her as he slowly came around beside her and him looking down at her again with the awfullest grin. "Annabelle" he said again with a small chuckle. "You know what I want!" he said smiling down at Annabelle. Have you ever felt frightened at something or someone? Annabelle was staring at him and he was now right in front of her. She couldn't move, she couldn't talk! All she could do was stare at him smiling at her. Her heart beating wildly in her chest. What was she going to do? It was as if time stood still around her and in this very moment everything became clear to her. She knew what she had to do but she was frightened, scared of what was going to happen, scared of what had already happened. What did I do? She thought to herself. All she could do was stare at him in the eyes, he was right there in front of her bent down grinning at her. She had seen him many times before but she never told anyone especially not her parents. She often wondered if she told someone maybe things would have been different. But it was too late now, she knew what she had to do. She watched as he circled around her chair grinning at her the whole time. She could feel her hair on end. Have you ever felt your hair stand, been alone with something or someone? Annabelle couldn't take it no longer, she quickly got up and ran out of the room. She didn't even look back to see him. Dr. Richards came to the house every day now. The situation was getting worse. Maybe I could have stopped it before but I was too scared then and now there was only one thing that I could do, only one person that I could talk to. "Father Stevens" Annabelle said as she stood in the middle of the church. "Father Stevens I have to talk to you" she slowly replied. "My child, please come sit" Father Stevens replied. "I'm not supposed to be here," Annabelle explained. "But I had to come, I had to talk to you!" she replied. "It's happening again," Father Stevens replied. "I tried to warn your Uncle Steven but he wouldn't listen," Father Stevens explained. "I thought that I could take care of this on my own father," Annabelle replied. "I realize now that I can not," Annabelle explained. "I'm worried about Conner, I'm worried about what he will do," Annabelle replied. "My child it's not Conner that I'm worried about, it's him" Father Stevens explained. "Father, I told you there were things that you might not understand. Things that I have seen and heard. I've seen Aunt Sarah, she comes to me" Annabelle explained. "That's not all. I haven't told anybody this. It's not the first time I have seen him but it's all getting worse now" Annabelle explained. "I was afraid of this Annabelle. Your Father doesn't want me coming around because of Dr. Richards. After the exorcism Dr. Richards had a talk with your father. Everything was blamed on Conner to make it all look like it was an accident." Father Stevens explained. "Your father decided that they would not come back to church but I knew something was wrong. Something was very wrong but your father pushed me out. Annabelle I tried to warn Conner but he wouldn't listen. He is still in that house. Dr Richards put him on medicine and kept him on it. He kept coming out and doing sessions with Conner until he believed everything that Dr. Richards had told him. Your Aunt Sarah didn't like the idea. Annabelle, it wasn't long after that your Aunt Sarah was found dead" Father Stevens explained. "What are you saying?" Annabelle asked. "Annabelle I can't prove anything and I am not for sure what really happened. All I know is that he is still in that house" Father Stevens said. "I have to help him," Annabelle replied. "You can't do this alone Annabelle, I have to come with you, it's the only way. What was started has to be finished" Father Stevens explained. "You must be prepared for what you will see and what you will hear" Father Stevens said. "You must not believe any of it, it's very important that you listen to me, do you understand?" Father Stevens asked. "Yes Father, I understand," Annabelle replied. "I just hope we are not too late" Father Stevens replied. I knew Conner was in trouble, we were all in trouble. As long as we were there we were not safe. I also knew that what Father Stevens said was correct, we had to finish what was started so many years ago. I still didn't tell Father Stevens everything, I was afraid that if I did he wouldn't have the strength to keep it all a secret. It was something that I was going to have to endure. It was my secret and so far the only weapon I had against him. It is what he wanted most and I wasn't going to give it to him, I couldn't. I was the only one that could help and I knew that. Have you ever been in a situation where you knew you were the only one. I was in that situation right now. At the same time I was scared to death. Everywhere I looked I could see them, at night it was worse. Can you feel them looking at you, following you, standing right behind you as if they can just reach out and grab you and there is nothing that you can do about it. For years I have been dealing with it, not able to tell anyone what was going on, what I saw or what I heard. The Farmhouse was worse. Everywhere you turned you could feel him watching you, staring at you. Have you ever been afraid to close your eyes when you went to bed? Have you ever covered your head when you heard them? The only thing to be heard was your own breath, but you know that they are there, watching you. Every shadow that you see pass by, or the ones that are standing behind you, or in the corner of the room. I can see them all. Some of them I would love to help and others I don't want to get near me. I didn't want him to get near me. I didn't have a choice this time. The worst thing about it is that I think he knew I didn't have a choice. The way he taunted me and grinned except this last time he was very clear at what his intentions were. I knew exactly what he wanted and I knew exactly what I had to do. Claireabelle was always such a sweet little girl. She always enjoyed the hide and go seek games that we would play and the berries that were picked. She loved when I would come over but I was so young then I didn't know what to do. I was fifthteen now and with everything happening again I knew that I could now do something about it. Dr. Richards was at the house when I arrived back home. He was talking with my uncle and I knew from the look on their face that something was going on but I didn't come alone. I didn't even make it to the porch before he was out the door yelling at me. "Why did you bring him here! I warned you about this!" Dr. Richards yelled. "This does not involve him. I told you that I was taking care of this!" he screamed. "Annabelle, Father Stevens already tried and he only made matters worse" Uncle Steven explained. "I have no choice but to allow Dr. Richards to take over," he explained. "Conner is not doing well and he needs a doctor that can help him." Uncle Steven said. "What is wrong with Conner!" I demanded to know. "Conner is not in the right state of mind Annabelle, it's best that you leave him alone" Dr. Richards said. "And as for you, you should not be here" Dr. Richards told the priest. "I think that you should leave at once," he replied. "No! Not this time. I failed once before and I will not let that happen again! I failed that little girl and I have a chance to finish what was started and I'm going to finish it" Father Stevens demanded. "That little girl was my daughter! And that boy is my son! I can not let you make the same mistake twice" Uncle Steven said. "You have to let him try Uncle Steven, you have to" I cried out. "I told Conner it wasn't his fault, you don't understand. I was there, I saw it all, everything. I can still hear him, calling my name. I hid Claireabelle like I always did and then I would hide and wait. I could hear him calling as he searched. It seemed like forever, then I heard her screaming and screaming. She wouldn't stop. We tried to make her stop but she wouldn't listen. She was so little and helpless. Conner just kept yelling at her to be quiet and when she didn't listen he slapped her across the face. We were only five years old then. His nails went right across her face. I can still remember the blood. It wasn't his fault, it wasn't his fault. I didn't know it then but something had taken over her. When you finally came down and saw what was happening Claireabelle was speaking like I have never heard her speak. She was saying things that I had never heard. She kept fighting you and scratching at you, I was so afraid. You took her to her room and Aunt Sarah Called Father Stevens. She wouldn't let us go in. She just kept holding us and telling us that everything was going to be alright. It felt like forever before the door was opened and Claireabelle seemed as if everything was alright. I know now that everything was not alright. He was still in the house, waiting for his time to come again. I wasn't allowed to come around for a while after that. I should have been here Uncle Steven" Annabelle explained. "Your right Annabelle, I should have never pushed you away" Uncle Steven replied. "But Conner needs my help now and I have to let Dr. Richards try," Uncle Steven explained. "Dr. Richards did try, he has been coming around here Poisoning his mind and I for one have had enough of it and will no longer tolerate it!" Father Stevens replied. "If you want this to end there is no doctor that can help you Steven" Father Stevens replied. "Now you can come with me and be of assistance or you can stand out here and argue amongst yourselves but that boy of yours needs my help now excuse me!" Father Stevens said as he went into the house. I was right behind him but it didn't take long before I knew that we were not welcome. Have you ever felt so afraid of something that you couldn't move? All you could do was stand there and breathe slowly like your breath was being taken from you. "Father something is not right!" I said. "I have felt this before, he is here" I said slowly. "Conner is upstairs in his room" my uncle replied. I didn't feel right. I knew that this time I had to go upstairs and help him, I was the only one that could. I was the one that had what he wanted. I slowly followed the priest up the stairs. I could feel every beat of my heart. I could hear every breath that I took. I tried to imagine that we were five years old again and that this was all just a nightmare and I was going to wake up soon but that was not the case. When we got to his room I felt a sigh of relief. It wasn't what I had imagined at all. Conner was asleep in his bed. The priest slowly walked over to his desk. Conner had left his Journal laying open. The priest began to slowly read through the pages. I stood and watched wondering what was written inside. I wondered if it was like taking a look inside his mind. Seeing all his thoughts and memories across every page but I didn't know. The priest just stood there staring at the page. I was starting to get nervous. "Father," I said quietly. Trying not to wake Conner up. "Why didn't you tell me" Father Stevens said as he slowly turned and looked at me. "What are you talking about" I asked as I walked over to the journal to take a look for myself. I couldn't believe what I was looking at. I quickly grabbed the journal and slammed it shut. Walking past the priest I headed downstairs and shoved the Journal into Dr. Richards chest. "This is your doing" I screamed at him. "You're trying to make Conner look like he is sick!" I screamed at him. "It's all your fault" I screamed as I started slapping him. "Annabelle" Uncle Steven yelled as he pulled me away from the doctor. "Annabelle! What is your problem" He demanded to know. "It's all his fault! Everything!" I screamed out. "If you don't believe me, take a look for yourself" I screamed as I left the room. I didn't want to believe it but it had to be true. Everything that I had discussed with Father Stevens and now seeing what was written inside that journal. I knew Conner, he was a little confused but it wasn't his fault. The more and more I thought about it the more I was convinced that it really was Dr. Richards' fault. I knew that Conner would never hurt anyone and the mere fact that it was suggested made me furious. I knew Conner didn't write the things that were inside that journal. "Annabelle" Father Stevens said as he walked up. I was swinging back and forth slowly on the old tire swing. "Annabelle, Dr. Richards gave Conner a sedative; he's going to be asleep for a while" Father Stevens said. "I know what was written isn't true. Annabelle we have to try to convince your uncle of that" Father Stevens explained. "The situation is worse than I thought." It sure was I thought to myself. Not only was the doctor trying to manipulate Conner but now he was trying to manipulate my uncle as well. I knew what the truth was and even though I wasn't around for a while I wasn't going to fall for what I was seeing or hearing. I had to try to find some way to get rid of Dr. Richards. I didn't know how I was going to or how I could help Conner. It was a time in my life that I felt helpless. There was so much that I wanted to say but I couldn't, not yet anyway. "Father, I don't think Dr. Richards is going to be leaving any time soon" I replied. "I got a confession I need to make. I watched Conner come home after talking with you. I went into my room and shut the door. I didn't want him to see me. He was looking and searching through the house. When he went down stairs I came out of my room and watched as he looked around. He started to go to the basement when my uncle came in. He saw me as he was leaving to go outside. I knew he would try again so I waited that night instead of going to sleep. After my uncle came up to check on him he went to his room to go to sleep. It was an hour after that I heard Conner open his room door. He checked to make sure my uncle was asleep then he went down stairs to the door of the basement. I made sure I stayed out of his sight so he would not see me. I followed him down to the basement and hid, he searched everywhere. When he was done he went back to his room. I know he was searching for her, just like when we played hide and go seek. Father I don't think Conner is taking his medicine. My Uncle gave him a pill that night and he should have been sleeping" I explained. "I think Conner is starting to figure out what is going on. I'm afraid that if he figures it out that he could be in more danger than we had anticipated" I replied. "Annabelle, everything is going to be alright. I don't know how yet but we will figure all this out. Right now let's focus on figuring out how we can best help Conner. We know the doctor is not going anywhere and I'm afraid he put Conner to sleep on purpose. I think Dr. Richards knows what we are up to" Father Stevens replied. "Well I might have told him that I was talking to you" I explained. "It doesn't really matter now. I'm going to my room." So many things had happened and I just needed to get a break from it all and I didn't want to see Dr. Richards anymore. I knew he wasn't going anywhere and I knew Father Stevens would be here as well. As long as Conner was sleeping this was my chance to get a little rest. I still felt uneasy when I went through the house. I'm sure you have felt uneasy too. It's mostly the old houses with the floors that squeak. The farmhouse had been around a long time. It was passed down from generation to generation and it wasn't going to be leaving our family any time soon. I wasn't in my room long and I found myself in a deep sleep. "Annabelle, Annabelle." I heard my name being called faintly. "Where are you, I don't see you" I replied. "Annabelle, Annabelle." My name was still being called. I looked around my room and then down the hall it was dark. "Where are you, I don't see you" I said again. I walked into the hall, everything was dark and I couldn't see anything. I just kept walking slowly into the darkness. "Where are you?" I replied again. "Annabelle!" I turned around, the voice was all around me. "Annabelle!" My heart was beating in my chest. "Aunt Sarah, is that you?" I asked. I could see her coming closer in the darkness. "Annabelle!" she kept calling out my name. "Annabelle, Annabelle, I can see you!" Her face was covered with scratches, she was reaching out for me. Trying to grab me. "Oh Annabelle, help me! I said help me Annabelle!" I was terrified, her arms just kept reaching for me, grabbing me as I pulled away. I closed my eyes tight. "Get away from me!" I yelled. "Annabelle, what's wrong?" I opened my eyes back up and Claireabelle was in front of me. The scratches pouring blood from her face. "What's wrong Annabelle? You don't like me? Why won't you help me" Claireabelle asked. "Get away from me, leave me alone, leave me alone" I screamed. "Annabelle, Annabelle, wake up!" Father Stevens yelled as he shook me. "Annabelle, It's just a dream" he said. My heart was pounding just like in my dream. "No Father, that felt real. I saw Aunt Sarah, and Claireabelle. She was calling for me. Reaching out for me, She had scratches on her face, when I closed my eyes Claireabelle was there, blood pouring down her face. She kept asking why won't you help me. Father, they were calling to me. I think they were trying to tell me something. Something is very wrong. I know it is" I explained. "Where is Conner" I asked suddenly. "Conner is alright" Father Stevens replied. "He is still sleeping. I've been keeping an eye on him. Your Uncle has been talking with Dr. Richards, they are downstairs. Annabelle, you must not believe the things that you hear and see" Father Stevens explained. "No Father, you don't understand, they were calling to me, I know they were!" I replied. "I have to help them, something is not right Father. I think Conner might be in trouble. Father you have to promise me that you will stay until all this is over. I can't do this alone." I replied. "Annabelle, I'm not leaving. I came to finish this and that is what I intend to do" Father Stevens explained. I knew something was seriously wrong. I could feel it in the gut of my stomach. I didn't know what was going to happen but I knew Conner was in trouble. I was sure that something bad had happened and I had to find out what. The more I thought about it the more I believed that Uncle Steven Kept me away for a reason. Somehow I knew that Dr. Richards was involved as well I didn't know how but I had to find out. I watched as Father Stevens blessed the house. When he was done upstairs I snuck into Conner's room. "Conner, Conner, wake up!" I whispered quietly as I shook him. "Conner I have to talk to you!" I replied. "Conner I need to know what happened to Aunt Sarah." Conner just lay there staring at me. "Conner, it's important," I said quietly. "Why does everyone keep asking me about mom?" he replied. "Conner do you remember anything at all, you must remember something" I said. "I know we don't talk much, so much has happened. So many things are so unclear but I know something bad has happened. Conner you were the only one here when Aunt Sarah died, you must remember something" I replied. "I've tried Annabelle, I can't remember anything. You were the one with Claireabelle's bracelet, you tell me what happened" Conner said. "I can see them Conner. I haven't told anyone. I gave the bracelet back to Claireabelle. I was sitting on my bed holding the bracelet when she came in. She sat beside my bed. We talked for a while then she was gone. Later that night I went downstairs to see if I could find her but she was gone. I came back upstairs and I heard you close your room door. I told you it wasn't your fault and went into my room. When I turned to close the door I could see Claireabelle going into your room. I stood and watched for a while but she never came back out. I went to check on you and you were on your bed. I was sure you were asleep so I left you alone and went to bed" I explained. "I had a dream tonight. They were calling to me, reaching out for me. Something is wrong Conner" I replied. "I come here every summer, I've never told you any of this. They need me here. Conner do you remember Claireabelle? She was your twin sister" I replied. Conner just lay there and stared at me. What did Dr. Richards do to him? Why can't he remember anything I thought to myself. "Conner do you remember what happened to Claireabelle?" I asked. It was no use he couldn't remember anything that had happened. Father Stevens told me that after the exorcism Claireabelle was never seen again. He also said that they blamed everything on Conner. I had to know what happened. Why were they calling out to me? I had spent a lot of time here on this farm but this was the worst feeling that I had ever had. The dream seemed so real and scary. I'm sure you have had one just like it. You can see their face and they are coming for you, reaching for you, blood dripping everywhere, grabbing your arms, calling your name. They are going to get you and there is nothing you can do about it. You always wake up in a cold sweat, heart pounding and are afraid to go back to sleep but was it all a dream or did it really happen. Everything seemed so real just like you were really there but you weren't there, you couldn't have been there. "Annabelle, do you hear that?" Conner asked. "Until now I have not been able to make it out but tonight it's very clear," Conner replied. "I can hear the screams, the cold shivering screams" he said. "I hear it every night but it's not Claireabelle. I can hear the screams of a woman Annabelle, don't you hear it?" Conner asked me again. "It's horrible, Annabelle I don't know what to do. Tell me you hear the screams!" Conner replied. "Conner, I don't hear anything," I replied. I could see the fear in Conner's eyes. I don't think I have ever seen him like this. "Annabelle, I need to tell you something. I have never gone to check, I have always been to afaid, too afraid of what I might see" Conner explained. "She's hurting Annabelle! Someone is hurting her! I don't know who she is. All I hear is screaming" Conner said. "Do you feel it Annabelle? It's cold all around me. I'm sick Annabelle, I must be sick" Conner replied. "Something is wrong! She's in trouble Annabelle, you must help her!" Conner screamed out. "Help her Annabelle!" he screamed again. "What's happening to you?" Annabelle asked as she slowly stepped away from Conner. "Annabelle what are you doing in here?" Dr. Richards asked as he went over to Conner. "She's screaming, I hear the screams" Conner shouted out again. "Conner, it's ok" Dr. Richards replied as he settled Conner back down. "Annabelle, I told you to stay away from Conner!" Dr. Richards yelled. "This is all your fault, you're upsetting him!" Conner was upset but it wasn't my fault. Everything was becoming clear to me now. How could Uncle Steven not have seen it before or maybe he did. I was starting to put all the pieces together. I think Conner was starting to as well. Dr. Richards had stopped all of that. He didn't want Conner to know what was happening. The more I watched, the more I was uncertain that Dr. Richards had acted alone. Before I was sure that it was all his fault but now after talking with Conner I had a different view on it all. I asked Father Stevens if he would walk outside with me. I needed to talk with him and Dr. Richards didn't want us around and I for one did not want him to hear what I had to say to Father Stevens. "Father, something bad happened here. Before now I was unsure of it but now I'm certain of it. After talking with Conner everything started to make sense to me. Father Dr. Richards didn't act alone like I suspected and Conner didn't write those things in that journal" I explained. "Annabelle, what are you saying?" Father Stevens asked. "I can't prove it yet Father but I think Uncle Steven is making Conner look sick. I don't know how I didn't see it before. I think it was Uncle Steven that wrote those things in that journal. Conner is starting to remember the things that have happened here and I think that Uncle Steven is trying to make him seem sick. He has been hearing her scream Father. I never told you this, for a long time I thought Conner was possessed. I even thought Claireabelle was possessed" Annabelle said. "I performed that exorcism Annabelle" Father Stevens said. "Yes you did Father but now I think it's time that you know everything" Annabelle explained. "I was so afraid of you being around here but now I realize that I need you here. Conner is not possessed. He has a split personality that I believe has been manipulated by Dr. Richards. For years he has been scaring me because I thought that it was all happening again and I didn't know what to do. It's been worse lately. He has come to my room and he is always smiling and grinning at me but I didn't understand it until now. After talking with Dr. Richards he told me that I knew what he wanted and he's right. I have what he wants. I'm the only one that can help Father" Annabelle explained. Conner is living the memory of his mother's death over and over. He is hearing her scream, he is searching for Claireabelle. He wants Claireabelle, he doesn't know that she is not here anymore. I did see her and I did talk to her Father except she's not alive" Annabelle replied. "I've kept this a secret, I've had to. I don't think what happened to Aunt Sarah was an accident Father. I think she found out what happened to Claireabelle and something very bad happened. I have to find out what happened and Conner is the only link between it all" Annabelle replied. "Annabelle, I believe you are right" Father Stevens said. "Father, there are more secrets that I have as well," Annabelle replied. "Uncle Steven was also so jealous. Conner Could never figure out why he acted so strangely. Aunt Sarah loved for me to come around, she thought of me as one of her own. When Claireabelle was born she named her after me and this upset Uncle Steven. I'm only three months older than the two of them. I wasn't supposed to tell anyone this Father but I have to. I can't bear to keep it a secret no longer. Father Uncle Steven is not their father." Annabelle explained. "Annabelle what are you saying?" Father Stevens asked. "Aunt Sarah did some really bad things Father and Uncle Steven found out. I think he did something to Claireabelle and when Aunt Sarah found out he killed her for it Father" Annabelle explained. "Annabelle, you must not tell anyone this" Father Stevens said. "I haven't Father" Annabelle replied. "Aunt Sarah told me long ago and I haven't told anyone. Now I think she is trying to reach back out to me Father. I think she is trying to warn me of something very bad" Annabelle said. "I don't know what happened here but I know that Conner must have seen or heard something. Dr. Richards is with him right now and I'm sure he is trying to keep Conner sedated. Father I didn't get the chance to get to know Claireabelle like I did Conner, at least not while she was alive. When she comes to me Father she reminds me a lot of Conner. Although she is sweet and kind there is another side to her" Annabelle explained. "It's much like

Conner, except I think that she is worse. Sometimes I wake up and she is staring down at me, it's scary. The room is dark and her hair is covering the scars. Sometimes she doesn't say anything. She just reaches out to me, I never knew why but now I think it's because she wants to tell me something. Father do you really think it's the house" Annabelle asked. "Annabelle, something has always seemed out of place here. Something is not right, you can feel it." Father Stevens said. "There is evil here Annabelle and although it may not be Conner there is something seriously wrong" Father Stevens said. "I miss Aunt Sarah Father," Annabelle replied. "It's not fair that the memories were taken from Conner and what happened to Aunt Sarah and Claireabelle are not fair either" Annabelle said. "No it's not fair Annabelle but we have to.." Father Stevens paused for a minute. "Annabelle did you hear that?" Father Stevens asked. "I need to go check on Conner, Excuse me" Father Stevens said. I was right behind him. Conner was my number one concern right now, I couldn't let anything happen. I could feel the air inside the house, it was cool. I stopped in the living as the priest went upstairs to check on Conner. Something wasn't right. There was a small flicker to the light. I stood staring at it for a minute. I walked slowly toward the light bulb that hung from the ceiling. Staring at the light that illuminated from the small bulb as each flicker made small flashing lights appear around the room. I walked slowly under the small bulb now staring up at it as the small flickers were now constant and flashing before my eyes. I reached up and as the tip of my finger touched the small bulb I heard him call out to me. Like many times before I could feel the pit of my gut start to tighten. The light was flickering faster as I slowly turned. "Conner, what are you doing" I asked. He stood staring at me with a grinning smile like he did many times before. "Conner," I said. The light suddenly slowly started flashing and I looked up at the bulb then back at Conner. The Basement door was opened behind him. The light went dark and lit back up again. "Conner!" I screamed out. I could see Claireabelle right behind him half her face covered with hair and small streaks of blood running down the other side of her face. Conner stood chuckling as he stared at me. "Conner!" I screamed out again as Claireabelle wrapped her arms around his face. I started to run towards him when the light bulb exploded sending shards of glass around the room. I screamed out frightened at the event and when I looked back up Conner was gone. "Annabelle, what's going on!" Father Stevens yelled. "Conner is not in his room, Dr. Richards is nowhere to be found and your Uncle is gone as well" he explained. "Conner was just here Father," Annabelle screamed. "It was Claireabelle Father, she was behind him, she grabbed him Father!" Annabelle said as her heart pounded in her chest. "What's happening Father? Why did Claireabelle grab him?" Annabelle asked. "You can't believe it Annabelle, don't believe the things you see or hear!" Father Stevens said. "It's all my fault, I should have stayed inside" Father Stevens said. "No Father, it's my fault, I brought you out of the house" Annabelle said. "I think he wanted us to leave the house. Something is wrong, I can feel it" Annabelle said as she went up to Conner's room. "Where is it?" Annabelle screamed. "It has to be here somewhere" she yelled. "Annabelle, what are you looking for?" Father Stevens asked. "Where is Conner's Journal?" Annabelle shouted. "It's not here!" she shouted again. "Father don't you see!" Annabelle asked. "The words I killed them were written in Conner's Journal!" she replied. "I think Claireabelle is trying to protect Conner," Annabelle explained. "Listen Father, do you hear that?" Annabelle said as she listened Closely. "I can hear him Father, he's calling my name, he's screaming for me to help him" Annabelle replied. "The lights Father, they are flickering again" Annabelle said. "She's trying to draw power from the house Annabelle," Father Stevens said. "Follow me Downstairs!" he shouted out. "Annabelle!" It was Aunt Sarah. I turned to look toward their room. "Aunt Sarah, is that really you?" I asked. "Annabelle," she said again. "Annabelle, don't listen to it" Father Stevens shouted. "Aunt Sarah" I called out running towards their room. Before I could reach her the door slammed shut in front of me. "NO!" I screamed out. I was pounding my fist on the door. Why was this happening? Where was Uncle Steven and Dr. Richards? "Annabelle, we have to go downstairs" Father Stevens said as he pulled me away from their room. "Annabelle stay close to me," he said. "I have to try to draw them out," he explained. My heart was still pounding. As Father Stevens began my attention was suddenly pulled to the basement door behind us. Claireabelle stood looking at me with her finger over her mouth. I couldn't say a word. Suddenly she turned toward the door and disappeared. I had forgotten about the basement door being open. Claireabelle always loved playing in the basement. Conner had to be down there. I turned toward the priest. He hadn't noticed and I decided that I would slip away while his back was turned. The light was dim on the staircase and I slowly stepped down. Was Dr. Richards and Uncle Steven down here I thought to myself. Would I find Claireabelle waiting for me or

Aunt Sarah. I knew they were not alive but I could see them, they were right in front of me. "Claireabelle," I called out quietly. The basement was dim but I could still see. "Claireabelle, I know you came down here" I said as my heart pounded in my chest. "Conner, are you down here" I asked quietly. I took each step slowly as I moved through the basement. In the far corner sat the chest I would always hide Claireabelle in. I could feel my breath shortening again and I could hardly swallow. "Claireabelle, are you here" I asked again as I stepped up to the chest. I had to open it. I had to know what or who was inside it. I reached slowly grabbing the handle trying to swallow again. "Claireabelle," I said quietly. I started pulling the handle up as I saw a black shadow run into the darkness. "Conner," I said as I released the handle. "Conner Is that you?" I asked. Have you ever been so scared to be alone? I knew I should have told Father Stevens that I was going to the basement but this was something that I had to do and I had to do it alone. "Claireabelle, are you down here?" I asked. I couldn't see anything, the light was too dim. I could barely breathe. It was as if my breath was stuck inside of me trying to escape. I knew something or someone was down here with me. I knew I had to know what was going on. "Conner, let me help you!" I quietly said. "It wasn't your fault Conner!" I explained. "It wasn't your fault!" I still couldn't see anything or hear anything. My heart was pounding in my chest now. Father Stevens must have known by now that I wasn't upstairs but the whole house was silent. Have you ever felt so alone? Do you feel them staring at you, I did. I turned and my foot kicked something on the floor, it startled me. It was too dim to see what it was. I reached down and picked it up. It was Conners Journal!

How did it end up in the basement? I slowly opened it up, my heart still pounding in my chest. It wasn't there, the page was ripped out! Where was the page at? What was going on? I quickly ran back upstairs. "Father Stevens!" I shouted. "Father Stevens! Where are you?" I screamed. I should have never left him. Where did he go? My heart was racing now. I ran through the house trying to find him, trying to find anyone. "Father Stevens! Conner! Uncle Steven!" I screamed out. "Dr. Richards where are you?" I screamed. "Annabelle!" I heard a voice behind me. I stopped suddenly. I stood there for a second listening to my heart pound. "Annabelle, don't you want to see me? I've been waiting for you!" I slowly turned and there she was. Father Stevens had told me not to believe anything I had seen or heard but she was right there in front of me. I was staring right at her. I could hear her speaking to me, she had to be real. "You have Conner's journal Annabelle" Aunt Sarah replied. "Can I see it?" she asked. I tried to remember what Father Stevens had told me as I gripped the journal tight in my hands. "Where is Conner?" I asked. "What did you do to him?" I asked again. "Annabelle" Aunt Sarah called out again. "NO! NO! You're not real!" I screamed out as I ran from her through the house. "Conner! Where are you?" I screamed. I closed my eyes tight and screamed out It's not your fault, It's not your fault over and over again. I kept screaming it out until I felt something grab me, I was still screaming I was scared. "Annabelle! Annabelle!" I heard my name screamed out. I slowly opened my eyes and it was Father Stevens he was shaking me and yelling my name out. "Annabelle, what's wrong?" Father Stevens asked. I looked around but didn't see anyone. I was still holding the journal in my hands. Why did Aunt Sarah want the journal, was she trying to tell me something I wondered. I slowly opened it up. It was different than before. "Father!" I replied as I looked up at him. "It's my handwriting in the journal!" I replied. I couldn't breathe again and my chest was starting to tighten. "I don't remember writing anything in the journal, Father what's going on?" I asked. "Annabelle, do you remember anything?" Father Stevens asked. "What are you talking about?" I asked. I slowly started reading the journal but I couldn't believe what I was seeing. Did I write this? I had to sit down. "Father what's going on I don't understand" I asked. "Nothing is making since," I replied. "Annabelle what do you remember?" Father Stevens asked again. "Father, you're scaring me, we were trying to find Conner and Uncle Steven and Dr. Richards. We heard them screaming, Father what happened?" I asked. Father Stevens stood there staring at me. It was really starting to scare me now. "Annabelle listen to me carefully," Father Stevens said. "You are remembering the events that took place a long time ago" Father Stevens said. I just sat there staring at him. The house was silent and dark. The journal was still in my hands. I looked down at the pages and started to read. "I remember it well, the farmhouse. I didn't want to go, my parents don't understand. They never do. It's my secrets. I never told them. I never want to" Annabelle read out loud. "I come here every summer," Annabelle told the priest. "I'm the only one that can help them," she replied. "Have you ever felt alone?" Annabelle asked Father Stevens. "I do all the time" she replied. "I know they are watching me. I can see them" Annabelle said. "They don't know they need help" she replied. Father Stevens just stood there staring at Annabelle. "Father, I know what happened,"

Annabelle said. "I know more than what you may think." she explained. "Father, I have to tell you everything," Annabelle replied. Father Stevens sat down next to Annabelle. "What are you talking about Annabelle?" Father Stevens asked. "This isn't going to make any sense to you right now Father but you have to listen to me" Annabelle explained. "It all started when I was little. I came here every summer. I would always play with Claireabelle. Uncle Steven was always so jealous of what was going on. He called Dr. Richards and tried to have him evaluate Claireabelle but Dr. Richards told him there was nothing wrong with her. That made him furious and he would often get in arguments with Aunt Sarah. That's when he called you. Aunt Sarah told me everything that happened. She knew how jealous he was and she didn't want me to get hurt. After the exorcism Claireabelle started acting strange she wouldn't listen she would always scream. He called Dr. Richards back and they got into a huge fight. Dr. Richards told him that he would try to help now that Uncle Steven had messed everything up. He started prescribing her medicine and that's when it happened. He overdosed Claireabelle and hid her body" Annabelle explained. "It's all right here in the journal." Father Stevens just looked at Annabelle in disbelief. "There's more," Annabelle replied. "Aunt Sarah found out what happened. There was a huge fight. Conner was the only one there, Father he could hear her screaming louder and louder but he was too afraid to go. He just sat there and covered his ears. Father, Uncle Steven was not alone that night. I believe Dr. Richards helped him to cover up the death of Claireabelle. He had been counseling Conner the whole time. Father, he didn't have a choice. He was made to cover the whole thing up. Father it got worse after that. After Aunt Sarah died Conner went crazy and that's when it happened. Uncle Steven wanted you to do a second exorcism on Conner" Annabelle explained. "What are you talking about Annabelle, I never performed anything on Conner" Father Stevens replied. "I know," Annabelle said. "Something very bad happened, Conner went crazy. There was nothing that Dr. Richards could do to help him. Conner did something very bad to Uncle Steven" Annabelle replied. "I come here every summer because I'm the only one that can help them. Dr. Richards has Conner now. I don't think there is anything that he can do to help him" Annabelle explained. "Father, I have to help them. This is never going to end until I find out the whole truth. They are stuck here and have been for a long time. I wanted to help but I didn't know how. Every year I always make it here. I'm always afraid Father. I know what I must do, I've known for a long time" Annabelle replied. "I have to go see Conner, I have to talk to him," Annabelle replied.

  I was scared, I still am. It's the secrets that are haunting me. Making the hairs on my neck stand. Making the pit of my gut turn. I will always see them, hear them. The shadows in the corner, noises in the night. I try to contain them but I can't. You hear them at night too. Moving all around you, touching you. Conner was in the institute now. I kept telling myself that everything was going to be alright. I kept going back to the farmhouse year after year trying to piece the puzzle together denying the things that had really happened. There was no denying it now. This had to be stopped. The truth had to be told.

"Annabelle" he slowly whispered. It was that smile, I couldn't stand seeing that smile. "Conner, I didn't want to come but I didn't have a choice. This has to end" Annabelle explained. "Have you seen Dr. Richards?" Conner asked. "He still comes to see me, even after everything that has happened" Conner chuckled. "It's kind of ironic after all these years." I didn't say anything. I couldn't help but to feel sorry for him. I know it wasn't his fault. I just stood there staring at him laughing. He had truly been driven crazy but still somewhere deep down inside him I knew that he knew the truth. I knew that he knew where Claireabelle was. I didn't know how but somehow I had to find out. I had to right the wrongs that had been done. I had to find her and bring her home. The events couldn't repeat themselves no more. I couldn't bear to just sit by and watch it no longer.

"Dr. Richards, it's been awhile." I sat in front of the desk watching as he stared at me. The silence made me nervous. "Annabelle," he replied. "You should not have come here," he said. "I know," I replied. "I didn't have a choice. Dr. Richards, you know why I am here." I watched as he stared at me in silence. "I knew this day was going to come," he finally said. "I tried to help him, Annabelle. You were there that night. So was Father Stevens. It was horrible I couldn't stop him, Annabelle I tried" Dr. Richards explained. "You can't beat yourself up over this, it's not your fault" Annabelle replied.

"Annabelle, that's not Conner in there. We lost him a long time ago I'm afraid" Dr. Richards replied. I didn't know what to say. "Annabelle, the things Conner did that night… You have to know that wasn't him" Dr. Richards said. "I know that's why I'm here," I replied. "Dr. Richards has he told you anything, anything at all?" I asked. "No Annabelle," Dr. Richards replied. "Conner's mind is lost." I knew this to be true. "Annabelle, there was nothing left of your uncle. That monster in there cut him open" Dr. Richards screamed. "There was nothing I could do to stop him. So much rage was trapped inside him. I've tried for so long to get his laughing out of my head, his smiling. All I could do was sit there, horrified by what I was seeing." I watched as small tear drops ran down Dr. Richard's face. I knew Conner had gone crazy, I knew why he did what he did. So many bad things had happened at the farmhouse and they just kept playing over and over again. In the end Uncle Steven got what he deserved but that didn't make it right. I couldn't help but to feel bad inside for Conner. There was nothing that I could do for him now except try to right what had gone wrong. I had to try to find Claireabelle, I had to make things right!

The farmhouse held many secrets, many I didn't want to uncover. I knew in order to find Claireabelle I had to do just that. I had to uncover what had happened in the past. I had asked the priest not to leave until everything was over. Something that I have never done before. "Father, I went to see Conner today," Annabelle said quietly. "I keep reading through this journal hoping that I have missed something. I miss her father. I can still see her, I can almost even feel her. She still calls out to me. I know she is asking for my help. I see her everytime I close my eyes and when I wake she's staring down at me but I feel so helpless father" Annabelle cried out. Do you hear her calling for you? Can you see the scars on her face? She will come after you too! Just wait, you will see. I did. Sometimes people don't know they need our help. That's what I was here for. I came every summer, to help them. Like a record playing over and over again never playing the last song. But this time it was different. This time the tears ran down my face. I felt an emptiness inside me. A void I couldn't fill. Claireabelle was gone and so was Aunt Sarah. Conner had lost himself through it all. Have you ever felt empty inside? That's the way I was feeling right now. "Annabelle" Father Stevens said. "Let me help you Annabelle." He slowly reached out to grab my hand. I just sat there for a moment in silence. "Father, you need to leave, they don't want you here anymore! Sometimes people don't know they need our help, Father. Something very bad happened. I'm sorry father it's time for you to go" Annabelle replied with tears running down her cheek. "I came to set things right this time. I can't be selfish anymore. I have to let you go!" Annabelle replied. "I have to let you all go!" Father Stevens just stared at Annabelle confused by what she was saying. "It was the screams Father. You ran to go check, it was horrible. The look in his eyes, you couldn't stop him. He couldn't take it anymore. Dr. Richards couldn't help him, he couldn't save him. You tried to stop him Father but you couldn't, I'm sorry" Annabelle explained. Father Stevens couldn't breath. All he could feel was the pain coming from his chest. "Sometimes people don't know they need help," Annabelle said quietly. Father Stevens couldn't breathe. He just sat holding his chest. "Annabelle," he said quietly looking down at his hand. "I'm sorry Father" she said as she watched the blood drip from his fingers. "It's time for you to go home" Annabelle said with tears in her eyes. I come here every summer, to help them but this time it was different. I walked up to the old tire swing it was swinging back and forth again. Claireabelle looked so beautiful in her dress as she sat there staring at me. I was going to miss the farmhouse. I knew I was supposed to help her, to find her. Maybe it was me being selfish but if I did I would never see her again. So I just stood there watching her swing.

  "It was the farmhouse, I remember it well. She didn't want to go. It was the secrets. I understand, I always have" he chuckled. "They will never find her and neither will you. She will come for you just like she came for me. Calling out your name, reaching for you, grabbing you. All you can see is the scars on her face, the blood dripping down" he said laughing hysterically. "Claireabelle, Claireabelle, she's coming for you!" Dr. Richards just sat watching him laughing and smiling. He couldn't help but to feel a small sense of relief as he stood up from his chair and walked away. Maybe I was being selfish. I know you see them out of the corner of your eye. I know the hair stands on the back of your neck. I can hear them, I do all the time. Can you see her? Claireabelle, she's coming for you!